THOMAS' ABC BOOK

THOMAS & FRIENDS™

Random House 🏠 **New York**

A Random House PICTUREBACK® Book

Photographs by Kenny McArthur, David Mitton, and Terry Permane

Thomas the Tank Engine & Friends™

CREATED BY BRITT ALLCROFT
Based on The Railway Series by The Reverend W Awdry.
© 2010 Gullane (Thomas) LLC.

Thomas the Tank Engine & Friends and Thomas & Friends are trademarks of Gullane (Thomas) Limited.
HIT and the HIT Entertainment logo are trademarks of HIT Entertainment Limited.

www.randomhouse.com/kids   www.thomasandfriends.com

Library of Congress Cataloging-in-Publication Data
Thomas' ABC book / photographs by Kenny McArthur, David Mitton, and Terry Permane for Britt Allcroft's production of Thomas the tank engine and friends. p. cm. "Based on the Railway series by the Rev. W. Awdry."
Summary: An alphabet book featuring Thomas the tank engine and his friends.
ISBN 978-0-679-89357-8 (pbk.)
[1. Railroads—Trains—Fiction. 2. Alphabet.] I. McArthur, Kenny, ill. II. Mitton, David, ill. III. Permane, Terry, ill. IV. Awdry, W. Railway series. V. Thomas the tank engine and friends. PZ7.T36965 1998 98-6233

Printed in the United States of America   July 1998   36

HiT™

HiT entertainment

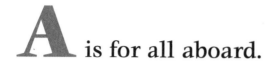

A is for all aboard.

"All Aboard!" calls Thomas the Tank Engine.

B is for Bertie the Bus.

Bertie is Thomas' friend. *Beep! Beep!*

C is for coaches.

Annie and Clarabel are Thomas' coaches.

D is for Diesel.

Doesn't Diesel look grumpy today?

E is for Edward.

Edward, a kind engine, helps everyone.

F is for freight cars.

"Trick-trock!" say the silly freight cars.

G is for Gordon.

Gordon is a big, strong engine. *Poop! Poop!*

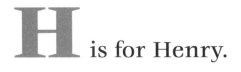

H is for Henry.

Here comes Henry under the bridge.

I is for important.

Trains do important work.

J is for James.

James is going on an exciting journey.

K is for kind. **L** is for little.

Kind little Edward is careful with freight cars.
Wheesh!

M is for men.

The men who drive the engine stand inside the cab.

N is for new.

Here's Henry with a new coat of paint.

O is for old-fashioned.

Toby the Tram Engine is old-fashioned but
very helpful.

P is for Percy.

Percy is the little green engine. *Peep! Peep!*

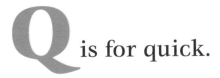**Q** is for quick.

James the Red Engine comes to a quick stop.

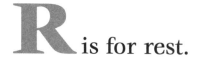**R** is for rest.

Thomas and Percy rest in the railway station.

S is for Sir Topham Hatt.

Sir Topham Hatt runs the railroad.

T is for tracks.

Terence tells Thomas about his tracks.

 **U** is for up.

Up on the bridge, Thomas chugs along happily.

V is for valley.

Thomas climbs out of the valley up the
steep hill.

W is for whoosh! **X** is for eXpress.

Whoosh! Gordon the Big Engine pulls the express.

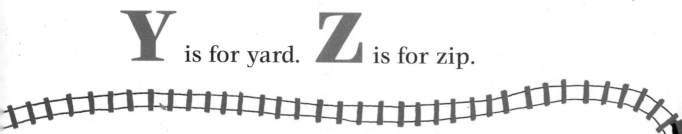

Y is for yard. **Z** is for zip.

Zip! Zip! Thomas is busy in the yard—pushing and pulling. Isn't he a Really Useful Engine?